LEABH...

MRS HIPPO'S
PIZZA
PARLOUR

VIVIAN FRENCH
Illustrated by
CLIVE SCRUTON

For all the lovely people at the Windsor Lodge Hotel – V. F.
For my nan, the best mince pie maker – C. S.

KINGFISHER

An imprint of Kingfisher Publications Plc
New Penderel House, 283-288 High Holborn
London WC1V 7HZ
www.kingfisherpub.com

This edition published by Kingfisher 2004
First published by Kingfisher 1999
2 4 6 8 10 9 7 5 3 1

Text copyright © Vivian French 1999
Illustrations copyright © Clive Scruton 1999

The moral right of the author and illustrator has been asserted.

A CIP catalogue record for this book
is available from the British Library

ISBN 0 7534 1037 0

Printed in India
1TR/0104/AJT/FR(FR)/115MA/F

Contents

Chapter One

It was two o'clock in the afternoon.

Mrs Hippo's Pizza Parlour

was empty.

Mrs Hippo was asleep.

William Hippo was reading

his comic. It was very quiet.

No one wanted to buy a pizza.

William put down his comic and
scratched his head.

He liked pizza.

His friends loved pizza.

So why didn't they come to

Mrs Hippo's Pizza Parlour?

Were they going somewhere

else instead?

Big Pig's Burger Bar gave away balloons.

Big Pig's Burger Bar had posters
all over town.

Maybe everyone was going there?

William's ears drooped.

If no one came to buy pizzas

there'd be no money.

No money meant no shopping . . .

and no shopping meant no bicycle

for William's birthday.

He'd seen a bicycle in the bicycle shop.

It was bright green, with a big bell.

William wanted that green bicycle.

He wanted it very badly.

RING!

It was the doorbell.

William ran to open the door.

"Hello!" said Ellie Bear.

"I've come to play!"

"Have you?" said William. "Why?"

Mrs Hippo opened one eye.

"Mother Bear's busy," she said.

"Come in, Ellie dear."

Ellie Bear took off her coat.

"Can I have a drink?" she asked.

William looked hopeful.

"Can we have biscuits, too?" he said.

"Two biscuits each," said Mrs Hippo.

"I haven't been shopping."

"Why not?" asked Ellie.

William leant towards Ellie.

"No one comes to buy pizzas any more,"
he whispered, "so we've got no money."

Mrs Hippo made hot chocolate

for Ellie and William.

She put four biscuits on a plate.

"Here you are, dearies," she said.

Then she went to make

herself a cup of tea.

Ellie drank her hot chocolate
very fast.

"I'm going to dunk my biscuits
in your chocolate," she told William.
She leant over the table . . .

William's hot chocolate spilt
everywhere.

"Oops!" said Ellie. "Sorry!"
William went to get a cloth.

When William came back the plate
was empty.

William put down the cloth with a
SPLATTT!

"Mum!" he yelled. "MUM!"

Mrs Hippo came hurrying in.

"What's the matter?" she asked.

"Ellie ate ALL the biscuits!"
said William.

Mrs Hippo looked at the mess.

"I think it's time we went out,"
she said.

"Let's go down to the sea."

"YES!" shouted Ellie and
William together.

Chapter Two

At the back of the pizza parlour

was a little yard.

In the yard was a motorbike.

A gleaming, glittering motorbike . . .

with a bright red sidecar.

The wheels were shiny silver.

The handlebars were wide.

The horn was LOUD.

"WOW!" said Ellie.

"That's MUCH better than a bicycle!"

William didn't answer.

He wanted a bright green bicycle

which he could ride by himself.

"Helmets on!" said Mrs Hippo.

"And hop inside!

BRRRRRRRRMMM!

Mrs Hippo revved up the motorbike.

"Hooray!" shouted Ellie.

"Go for it, Mum!" shouted William.

BRRRRRRRRRRRRMMM!

They were off!

Down the road went the bike.
PARP! PARP!

They waved to little Tilly Tiger
and her dad at the bus stop.

Under the bridge.

PARP! PARP!

They waved to the Giraffe family
on their tricycles.

Right at the garage.

PARP! PARP!

They waved to the

monkey mechanics.

Left at the shops.

PARP! PARP!

They waved to Auntie Elephant.

Auntie Elephant was having

too much trouble with her

shopping trolley to wave back.

They zoomed on down to the sea.

"WHEEEEEEEEEEEEEE!!"
yelled Ellie and William.

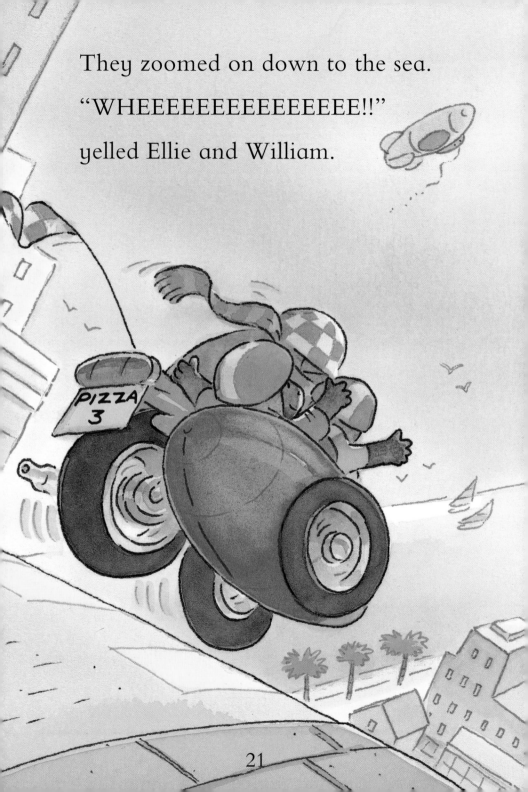

Mrs Hippo roared along the

sea road.

She roared over the promenade,

and down to the sand.

Then she stopped.

"WOW!" said Ellie, as she got out.

"That was FUN!"

Chapter Three

"Now," said Mrs Hippo.

"What about making a sandcastle?"

"NO!" said Ellie. "I want to go for

another ride!"

"Me too," said William.

Ellie looked at the smooth yellow sand.

"Can we ride on the sand?"

she asked.

"Well . . ." said Mrs Hippo.

"There's no one here," said Ellie.

"We could make tracks!" said William.

Ellie jumped up. "We could write

ELLIE in the sand!"

"YES!" William jumped up too.

"EVERYONE will see it!" said Ellie.

"They'll see it on the moon!"

Ellie and William rushed back into the sidecar.

Mrs Hippo climbed onto the motorbike.

BRRRRRRRRRRRRMMM!

They were off.

25

First of all they wrote ELLIE

in the sand.

"That's good," said Ellie. "Now

write William."

"No," said William.

"Why not?" asked Ellie.

"I've had an idea," William said.

His eyes were shining.

"An idea about the pizza parlour!

It's a MUCH better idea than

Big Pig's posters!"

He whispered in Mrs Hippo's ear.

Mrs Hippo nodded . . .

"Write it BIG, Mum," William told her.

Mrs Hippo got ready.

BRRRRRRRRRRRRMMM!!

Right across the sand they roared.

Up and down,

and round and round.

At last Mrs Hippo stopped.

They all looked at the sand.

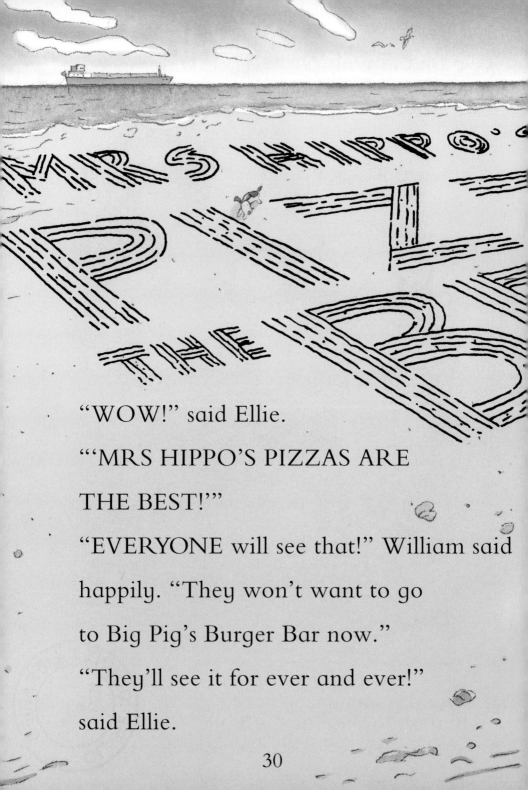

MRS HIPPO'S PIZZA THE B

"WOW!" said Ellie.

"'MRS HIPPO'S PIZZAS ARE
THE BEST!'"

"EVERYONE will see that!" William said
happily. "They won't want to go
to Big Pig's Burger Bar now."

"They'll see it for ever and ever!"
said Ellie.

"No, dearie," said Mrs Hippo.

"The tide will come in tonight.

It will wash the sand all clean and

smooth again."

"Oh," said Ellie. Then she smiled.

"We could do it again tomorrow!"

"Maybe," said Mrs Hippo.

"But now we'd better be going home."

"Can we have an ice cream?"

asked Ellie.

Mrs Hippo shook her head.

"I'm sorry, dearie," she said.

"Look! Not even a penny in my purse!"

William looked sad again.

He thought about his birthday.

They'd have to sell lots and LOTS

of pizzas to make enough money for

a green bicycle.

A bright green bicycle with a big bell.

"What's the matter, William?"

asked Ellie.

"Nothing," said William.

"We'll go home the long way,"

said Mrs Hippo. "That'll cheer us all up!"

Chapter Four

It was five o'clock when they

got home.

"Mum!" said William.

"Look at all those people outside

our pizza parlour!"

"Dear me," said Mrs Hippo.

"I think they're waiting to come in!"

"What do they want?" asked Ellie.

"PIZZAS!" said William.

"HOORAY!"

They all hurried inside.

"Come on, Ellie!" said William.

"We've got things to do!"

"I'll help," said Ellie. "I like helping!"

Mrs Hippo lit the oven.

Then she grated the cheese . . .

and cut up the onions . . .

and sliced the mushrooms . . .

and diced the peppers.

William rolled out the pizza dough.

And Ellie helped, too.

She tidied the tables . . .

and brushed the floor . . .

and shook the ketchup bottle . . .

"Ellie," said Mrs Hippo.

"Yes?" said Ellie.

Mrs Hippo took away the ketchup bottle.

"Wouldn't you like to read William's comic?"

"No," said Ellie. "I like helping."

39

At half past five Mrs Hippo opened
the pizza parlour door.

"Do come in," she said.

"We saw your sign on the sand,"
said Tilly Tiger.

"So did I!" said Auntie Elephant.

"We did, too!" said Grandpa Giraffe.

"Don't want burgers any more!"

said Baby Giraffe.

"We love pizza!" said the monkeys.

"That's right!" everybody said.

"We LOVE pizza!"

Mrs Hippo and William
worked and worked.
Ellie went on helping.

At half past seven Mother Bear came
into the pizza parlour.
"Oh my!" she said. "You ARE busy!"
"Yes," puffed Mrs Hippo, "we are!"
Ellie gave her mother a big hug.
"We wrote, 'Mrs Hippo's Pizzas
are the Best!' in the sand and now
everybody's come to see!"

"YES!" said William. "And they all want LOTS and LOTS of pizzas!"
Mrs Hippo nodded. "Tomorrow I'm cooking a new Seaside Special! – so they're all going to come back, and bring their friends!"
"Goodness!" said Mother Bear.

"We'd love to see Ellie again,"
said Mrs Hippo. "What about Sunday?"
"That's my birthday!" said William.
"That's right," said Mrs Hippo.
"Ellie can come for birthday tea
and see your present!"
And she winked at Ellie, and gave
William a big hug.

Chapter Five

On Sunday, Ellie rang the doorbell.

RING!

William opened the door.

"Hi!" said Ellie. "Where's your
present from your Mum?"

"Come and see," said William.

And there in the middle of the

pizza parlour was . . .

the bright green bicycle with a big bell.

And what did they have for tea?

SPECIAL BIRTHDAY PIZZA!

About the Author and Illustrator

Vivian French used to work in the theatre, acting and writing plays. She has written lots of books for children and often visits schools and libraries to tell her stories. She and Clive Scruton have been friends for a long time. They first thought up the story of *Mrs Hippo's Pizza Parlour* while sitting together on a beach . . . eating pizza! Vivian French's other books for Kingfisher include *Tiger and the Temper Tantrum* and *Tiger and the New Baby*.

Clive Scruton wanted to be either Spiderman or a cosmonaut when he was a child. But then he discovered he could draw – and has since illustrated over fifty books for children. Now he is married and lives in a house surrounded by his children, their rabbits and his own comics and robots. Clive often goes on bicycle rides . . . but what he really wants is a bright red motorbike with a sidecar!

Tips for Beginner Readers

1. Think about the cover and the title of the book. What do you think it will be about? While you are reading, think about what might happen next and why.

2. As you read, ask yourself if what you're reading makes sense. If it doesn't, try rereading or look at the pictures for clues.

3. If there is a word that you do not know, look carefully at the letters, sounds, and word parts that you do know. Blend the sounds to read the word. Is this a word you know? Does it make sense in the sentence?

4. Think about the characters, where the story takes place, and the problems the characters in the story faced. What are the important ideas in the beginning, middle and end of the story?

5. Ask yourself questions like:
Did you like the story?
Why or why not?
How did the author make it fun to read?
How well did you understand it?

Maybe you can understand the story better if you read it again!